The Supreme Tea of All Teas
by R.S. Kellogg

Copyright Information

The Supreme Tea of All Teas

Copyright © 2021 by R.S. Kellogg

Published by Rebecca Kellogg International

Cover and Layout copyright © 2021 by Rebecca Kellogg International

Cover design by Rebecca Kellogg/Rebecca Kellogg International

Cover art copyright © grandfailure/Depositphotos

Author photo on print edition by Lisa Collins.

This book is licensed for your personal enjoyment only. All rights reserved. This is a work of fiction. All characters and events portrayed in this book are fictional, and any resemblance to real people or incidents is purely coincidental. This book, or parts thereof, may not be reproduced in any form without permission.

Introduction

The barrier to entry for some professions can quite unique in terms of the path that must be walked in order to obtain the job.

I grew up in a university community and have known a great number of academics in my time.

The stress I've witnessed some people going through to try and get tenure can be really intense.

I'd imagine that at a magical university, the pressure around getting tenure may be even more challenging.

At Borealis University, up in the hills to the west of the city of Breadcove Bay, many students come to learn scholastics, magic, and how to navigate their country of Langasee and the world beyond.

Borealis University is also the employer of choice for the young teacher Shanning, whom this story is about.

After years of learning the ropes, completing advanced studies, and finishing up his student teaching, he now faces his ultimate test, with potential full employment on the line.

The final test to get hired varies based off of who administers the test.

Shanning gets to take his test with the Luminator, a dicey option when it comes to test administration.

She herself creates a wide range of different tests for different teaching applicants. Their difficulty level and complexity depends on her mood of the day and her attitude toward the particular candidate in question.

I rather think she has a good nose for sniffing out who will be a good fit for the staff of the university, though; as well as who will be a good teacher for the students.

Let's see how Shanning does.

The Supreme Teas of all Tea

by R. S. Kellogg

Shanning sat diagonally across his great chair, and stared despondently at the table before him.

He was sitting in the middle of the Luminator's vast workroom at Borealis University—its spectacular carved back doors led to a path that went directly into the forest—and he was staring at four small cups of tea.

It was early on a cold winter's morning, and Shanning wore a thick woolen wrap to keep his angular shoulders warm from the frigid temperatures of the Arctic climate.

He sat on a double-folded wool blanket to pad the chair and give some comfort to his bony body.

Despite the blanket, the wrap, and the five layers that he wore, Shanning shivered in the cold morning, and wrapped his scarf a little more snugly under his chin. His fingertips felt numb, and his nose was cold—he kept sniffling.

Shanning wore two pairs of the thickest socks he could buy; he also wore fingerless gloves, even though he was indoors and a large fire crackled merrily in the Luminator's workroom, sending heat throughout the well-designed room.

Herbs hung from the ceiling in dried bunches and bags, and row after row of shelving held all kinds of exotic spices, oils, and other ingredients of the finest quality, sourced from all over the Golden Circle of trading cities from the sea, the declining but still spectacular cities across the great land of Langasee, and the vast Mer civilization under the ocean.

The air smelled of a pleasant blend of spices and other aromas—cinnamon, and lavender, and the unmistakable sharp seaweedy notes of mermaid salve—the whole space fairly hummed with possibility and the electric energy of creative potential just waiting to be unleashed.

Many who lived in Breadcove Bay and even further north had a habit of putting on weight to help combat the freeze, the cold, and the frost.

Shanning had never been able to keep much weight on.

Today, as on every day, he wore a belt that he had added two holes to himself and cinched tight in order to keep up his pants.

On any other teacher at Borealis, Shanning's pants would have been tight.

But on Shanning, they looked unrealistically baggy.

He envied the old-school teachers, who wore robes and cloaks—clothes that didn't require any belts.

But he was the youngest person on the teaching staff; and he was aware that were he to wear the robes and cloaks of the elder teachers, he'd come across as pretentious and above his station.

He looked forward to passing his fortieth birthday, when robes and cloaks would be accessible as his wardrobe of choice without leading to a host of arched eyebrows.

And for now, he put up with the constriction of a belt cinched too tightly across his waist, simply to keep up the rough pants he wore—pants made of the cheapest material which he could get away with and still look respectable, getting by on his beginning salary.

The Luminator sat across the table from Shanning.

She was a tall woman with a pale face, thick black hair tied back with a silk black ribbon, and the most eerily pale eyes—one green and one blue. She wore a golden pendant bearing the image of a delicate phoenix on a long necklace.

The Luminator wore a long dark purple robe, which for most faculty members would mark them as being past forty, though as far as Shanning had ever known, the Luminator had worn robes for as long as he'd been aware of her. And she looked quite young, perhaps barely older than himself.

He envied her status, her robe, and her workroom, but mainly he felt very grateful to be here this morning.

Today was the day in which Shanning would have the final test to be accepted for a full-rank position and become tenured faculty.

Even seated, the Luminator had an inch or two on Shanning.

She waved her hand toward the four small, white cups which sat on the table in front of him. "Honorable Shanning," she said, and nodded at him.

Shanning tensed. His moment had arrived.

"Yes, Honorable Luminator?" he asked, nodding at her in return.

He sniffled again. Really, having a bit of a drippy nose on the day of his final test was a little bit obnoxious.

He wished that this morning he had taken the health-boosting potion which his grandmother had sent him with his birthday care package the previous month. It would have gone a long way to ease his confidence if he hadn't been worried that his nose would run.

"Today, your test is easy," the Luminator said sternly.

Shanning nodded again, attempting to look nonchalant.

The Luminator was one of the most powerful and mysterious people on a campus full of powerful and mysterious people.

He was hoping that he was coming across as confident and ready for the test.

"Before you, we have four cups of tea," the Luminator said, her voice melodic but almost detached, very professional and brisk. "Your task is to sip each one and to determine which is the Supreme Tea of all Teas."

Shanning glanced at her. "That's it?"

She stared back at him with her blue eye and her green eye, as steadily as a cat. "Yes."

Shanning frowned. "Is there a particular parameter that helps us determine which among these teas would be the Supreme Tea of all Teas?" he asked her.

She smiled, still watching him closely. "That is for you to tell me," she said.

Ah.

A test of his discretion and judgment.

He tipped his head to one side, and studied the cups.

They were arranged on the dark wooden table in a pattern like a square.

Steam rose from above the rims of the cups, and they presented him with warm scents of a variety of flavors.

The one on the top left had a faint blue-green tint, with a small bit of the debris of tea-leaves at the bottom.

The one on the top right was the palest shade of pink. That one had the most steam.

Bottom left was a muddy shade of brown.

And bottom right was a pleasant tone of red, but it wasn't a steady shade of red. Shanning looked at it closely and saw that its colors shifted a bit between a range of warm hues as he moved his head this way and that and the liquid caught the light. Red, orange, a hint of gold.

Right.

Pick the Supreme Tea of all Teas.

He raised his eyebrows.

It felt like a deceptively simple task.

He had already passed rounds and rounds to get here— calculations, elixirs, managing creatures. Negotiating with snow elves, passing a written exam on classroom supply chain protocols as it applied to the university, and perhaps most daunting of all: he had passed his student teaching rounds.

It had been a lot, all that he had done so far as a teacher, plus all that he had learned during his long years before that as a student.

Yet none of this, as he sat there and stared at the four white cups, brought him any sudden insights about what might constitute the Supreme Tea of all Teas.

He sighed.

This was probably going to be one of those exploratory exercises that some of the younger faculty members were so fond of.

The Luminator hadn't started wearing robes so very long ago.

He glanced at her one last time.

She raised an eyebrow, "Take all the time you need, but remember that you'll still be expected to be read to teach your noontime class."

With that reassuring encouragement, Shanning took a deep breath, steadied himself, and gingerly picked up the first cup.

The blue-green tint had a bit of a minty smell, with something else, and as he gently tipped it this way and that, studying the color of the tea, he saw the leaves at the bottom shift slowly to the side.

He took a deep sniff in, and appreciated how the warmth from the cup soothed his nose.

It seemed to bring him in mind of a memory—of having been a small child, playing at a beach near the docks while his brothers tussled in the sand.

Slowly, he raised the cup to his lips.

He took a deep sip.

The room wavered.

He set the cup down as the sensation of powerful waves rose around him.

He sensed water rise up around him, and the imagery was so strong that he held his breath. His hair floated in the water, his eyes stung, and he saw a mermaid with long blonde hair which was tied back, and a pearl necklace that floated in the water as she drifted up to his level and stared at him with a piercing gaze of narrow blue eyes.

Her long, powerful tail trailed in the water behind her, and he had a moment of shocked realization.

He had never seen a mermaid in the water before—in her home turf.

The few times in which he'd seen one near the tide, they'd always been coyly melodic, and quick to dive away when a crowd of people came near.

But this one, in her home terrain, was unquestionably powerful.

The mermaid brushed his arm with her hand, as if assessing who he was and what he might be doing in her realm.

Her touch was jolting, as though all the blood within him recognized it was akin to water, and had found a joyous, powerful, affirming friend.

She smiled, in a most unsettling way. She looked hungry.

Shanning's heart pounded.

His breath ran out, and he took a compulsive breath.

The sense of water ripped away from him, and with a shock he realized he was back in the Luminator's workroom.

Again freezing.

He coughed, and shook himself.

The Luminator smiled, and it was also an unsettling smile.

"Interesting," she said.

She glanced at his arm.

Shanning looked down, to see that where the mermaid had touched him there was a damp spot on his sleeve.

He took a shuddering breath. "That's like no tea I've ever had before."

The Luminator looked stern. "The task, Honorable Shanning, is that you must find the one which is the Supreme Tea of all Teas."

Shanning nodded. "As you say," he replied, and rubbed the back of his head. Was this all going to be element stuff then? It could make for a draining morning. "As you say," he repeated.

He carefully picked up the second cup.

The palest of pinks met his gaze within the second cup. Steam wafted from the top of the cup and warmed his nose as he lifted it to take a whiff of the aroma.

It smelled oddly of cream, and roses, but also somehow of butterflies, which was a scent Shanning had never considered that he may know.

But there it was.

On the confirming sniff, Shanning definitely smelled butterflies.

He carefully lifted the cup to his lips, and took a delicate sip.

Instantly, the room fell away, and he was falling through the air, turning and spinning this way and that.

Great sky and clouds were all around him, as far as he could see in any direction: blue and white, and shades of gray.

With a great shout he realized that the earth was nowhere to be seen beneath him, and instead great figures were twirling around him in the air.

He gazed into the wide dark eyes of a being filled with air, which spun around him and tossed him higher up toward the sky.

Another being caught him there, and embraced him as if in a hug.

Shanning flipped vertically and ended up sideways.

"I don't know what you are," he said, the words getting torn from his lips. "But you're very strong."

He could have sworn that he heard the laughter of gale-force winds.

Shanning felt terrified, and also like he had a headache.

How was he to step back out of this?

He tried wiggling his fingers, but he was still falling, the plaything of the winds.

"I have no power here," he conceded.

The winds chortled, and the scene vanished, and Shanning was once again sitting on the hard-but-padded surface of the chair in the Luminator's workroom.

He coughed, and he realized his scarf was badly tangled.

With shaking hands, he carefully straightened his scarf, the cup with the pink tea sitting off to one side.

Was he supposed to pick the tea that was the most powerful? Because he'd be hard pressed to weigh the relative strengths and merits of the mermaid and the air sprites.

Good Skies, those had been huge air sprites.

Great Frost Queen, he still had two cups to go.

He avoided looking at the Luminator as he picked up the third cup.

His fingers were still mildly trembling.

This third cup held liquid that was a muddy shade of brown, and Shanning braced himself.

Was he to end up buried under the earth once he drank this cup?

The Luminator certainly had an odd sense of humor, he thought darkly.

There was nothing for it.

He tried to consciously relax his shoulders before he raised the cup to his mouth and took the tiniest of sips.

He was aware he set the cup on the table as found himself sitting on a cold, hard dirt surface, under a canopy of leaves.

The air smelled of dirt, and lichen, and of the green-y smell of living wood.

A grin broke out across his face.

The space felt peaceful.

He had never seen such lushness.

The air was cold but he was surrounded but the most enormous trees, huge trunks wider than the fattest teacher at his university, long limbs waving like arms toward the sky.

Birdsong unfamiliar to him rang out through the trees, and he heard the rustling of branches as small creatures ran through the leafy canopy.

Unbelievably, he heard the trees making sounds—talking to each other—their roots growing deep, making the sounds of a deep-stringed instrument, their branches as they reached toward the stars interacting with what sounded like a hidden symphony of joy.

You're welcome to sit here, little stranger, he heard the deep voice of a great tree say, and Shanning sat back on his hands with the most incredulous smile on his face.

He took a deep sigh in, and gazed up at the sky.

Above him the stars shone down.

Overall, the place filled him with a vast sense of life.

He gave a shuddering sigh of release, and suddenly the landscape fell away.

He was back on the chair in the Luminator's workroom. He put his hands on the table to steady himself after the sudden shift, and saw that there was dirt on his fingers.

Pulling his handkerchief from his pocket, he wiped his fingers clean, and dabbed at his frigid nose.

"Only one cup left to go," he said, in a hopeful, cheerful voice, looking at the stern face of the Luminator, who was looking at his dirty handkerchief with a closed expression.

He carefully picked up the last cup—the shifting shades of red, orange, a hint of gold.

He stared at it.

He'd experienced water, air, and earth, which meant the only thing left was . . .

"Fire," he whispered, staring into the depths of the cup.

Was he really going to emerge in an inferno?

He glanced at the Luminator, who remained expressionless.

Shanning hadn't *heard* of previous teachers becoming scorched or incinerated during their final test for full employment, but he also knew that Borealis University could be a strange and sometimes punishing place.

Things did happen, sometimes, which were inexplicable.

People did have odd magical accidents.

But was he truly to be transported into the realm of fire?

Water had made his sleeve wet, and Air had disheveled his scarf. Earth had left his hands with dirt.

Fire . . .

He mentally calculated the distance to the infirmary, should he need it, and also mentally calculated how much he desired this job.

He nodded to himself.

He could do this.

One tiny sip, a few moments in a blaze, the correct identification of the Supreme Tea of all Teas, and he could have this job.

He tapped his foot against the floor. He wasn't sure he was up for this.

"You're stalling," the Luminator observed.

He shook himself. "You're right," he said.

He delicately raised the cup to his lips, staring first at the red shifting tones of the tea—which smelled of raspberry and hot lemon—and then glancing at the Luminator, who possibly looked a little bit fascinated as she kept a close eye on him.

He wasn't sure if she was about to watch him go up in flames, but he closed his eyes, and took a sip of the liquid.

Again, the room fell away.

He stood in a burning mass of flames.

The heat was formidable—he could feel the blast of the warmth from all around him almost forcibly pushing against his skin—but in here he also felt—deliciously, shockingly, fully warm.

The warmth ran through him, causing him to take a deep sigh in—his lungs didn't scorch!

He noticed the edge of his scarf was on fire, and shrugged to himself that something like this was to be expected.

Shanning stood in the flames for a good long time, soaking in the warmth, allowing it to permeate every fiber of his clothing, every piece of his body and soul.

It just felt so good to be warm.

He sensed some sort of intelligence to the flames, but he couldn't place a being or figure—in all the other spaces, he'd seen an elemental, or heard or talked to some essence.

"Hello?" he called, his words lost to the flicker of fire. "Is anyone there?"

He walked around a bit, and saw no one.

Finally, he sat down, on the hot parched earth that smelled of an oven, waiting, expecting someone to come. Simply feeling exultantly happy to sit, and be warm.

Finally, through the flames, he saw a tall figure come.

He stood up.

It was the Luminator.

Her black hair was now a striking shade of red, and an aura of power radiated from her eyes.

Her purple robe had become white.

"You've been in this too long," she said. "You need to come back to the workroom if you ever want to be free of here."

He startled. "It just feels so good to be warm," he said.

She nodded sympathetically. "If you don't leave the world of the tea, it will burn out your life force. And then you'll be dead. And you won't pass your test."

He chuckled. "Very well," he said.

This time, he noticed that he could consciously let go of the realm the tea took him to, letting the edges of the world of fire go.

The cold air of the Luminator's office hit him like a shock of a wall.

He gasped with the sheer difference, and wrapped his arms around himself.

"Look at you," the Luminator said.

She was still shifting—he stared at her for a moment and watched, as the red faded from her hair—it was returning to black. And the white of her tunic was darkening to its customary purple.

Not wanting to be rude and stare, Shanning then looked down at himself.

His hands felt as if they'd had just a minor sunburn.

He glanced down at his clothing, and saw that there were many singed spots across his pants and the arms of his tunic.

"Don't stay in there so long if you go again," said the Luminator.

He snorted.

He looked back at her.

She was primly back to normal now: Black hair, purple tunic, professional demeanor.

"Can you tell me then," she said, "Which one is the Supreme Tea of all Teas."

Shanning picked his words carefully. "I'd have to say, Honorable Luminator, that they are all equally powerful in their own way." He paused, searching within himself, seeking for the knowledge he understood that this assignment called on him to retrieve from within himself. "But I suspect the deeper question is—which tea for me is the Supreme Tea of all Teas. And I'd have to say the answer to that question is Fire. The red one. Because it was so blasted warm." He smiled at the memory. "I didn't even mind the singed clothing," he said. A tremendous acknowledgment for a teacher on a budget.

She laughed softly. "We'll have to get you a robe early," she said. "They don't burn, you know, and typically teachers don't see elementals in the realms invoked by the teas until they're a little further on—probably around age forty or so."

Shanning raised his eyebrows. Ah. One mystery behind the robes was explained.

"So I've passed?" he asked.

"You've passed," she said. "You'll need to go to the university stores and get a new outfit before your first class, though. I can write you a note to grant you a robe."

He laughed to himself, delighted.

He'd passed!

His salary would go up.

He'd get to wear a robe early, and not have to worry about too-big pants and an inconvenient belt anymore.

And, he could afford the new clothes without needing to eat substandard food for a week.

"I thought I'd see an elemental in the fire realm," he told the Luminator, as she walked him toward the door of her workroom. He could tell that he smelled of singed clothing. He'd need to bathe before his first class. "I saw an elemental everywhere else but not there. I was kind of disappointed that it didn't happen!"

    The Luminator stared at him. "Who says you didn't see one?" she asked, one green eye and one blue eye looking at him like a cat, the golden pendant on her chain bearing the image of a phoenix.

About the Author:

R.S. Kellogg writes in the fantasy Breadcove Bay series, as well as exploring other story worlds and non-fiction topics.

For more information about future books and other projects, please visit www.rskellogg.com.

Sign up for the RKI newsletter to receive updates on new releases, additional content, and more! Go to rskellogg.com.

Made in the USA
Columbia, SC
15 July 2021